Moving

Anita Ganeri

Watts Books
London • New York • Sydney

© 1994 Watts Books

Watts Books
96 Leonard Street
London EC2A 4RH

Franklin Watts Australia
14 Mars Road
Lane Cove
NSW 2066

UK ISBN: 0 7496 1516 8

Dewey Decimal Classification 612.7

10 9 8 7 6 5 4 3 2 1

Series editor: Pippa Pollard
Editor: Jane Walker
Design: Sally Boothroyd
Artwork: Bob Harvey
Cover artwork: Helen Parsley
Photo research: Alison Renwick

A CIP catalogue record for this book
is available from the British Library

Printed in Italy by G. Canale and C. SpA

Contents

How do you move?	3
Your skeleton	4
What are bones made of?	6
Joints	8
Inside a joint	10
Your skull	12
Your backbone	14
Main muscles	16
Muscles at work	18
Inside a muscle	20
Fuel for muscles	22
Hands and arms	24
Legs and feet	26
Pulling faces	28
Things to do	30
Glossary	31
Index	32

How do you move?

What happens to your body when you move? Your brain, nerves, muscles and bones all work together to make you walk, run or jump. You can also make smaller movements, such as a smile or a frown. You are always moving, even when you are asleep. Your heart and lungs move inside you to keep you alive. How many times have you moved since you started reading this book?

▽ These runners can move very fast.

3

Your skeleton

There is a strong, hard framework of bones inside your body. This is called your **skeleton**. It holds your body up and stops it collapsing in a heap. Your skeleton also helps you to move. There are muscles fixed to the bones. They pull on different parts of your body to move them. Your skeleton also protects delicate parts of your body.

▽Your smallest bones are deep inside your ears. There are three in each ear, called the hammer, anvil and stirrup. These bones help you hear.

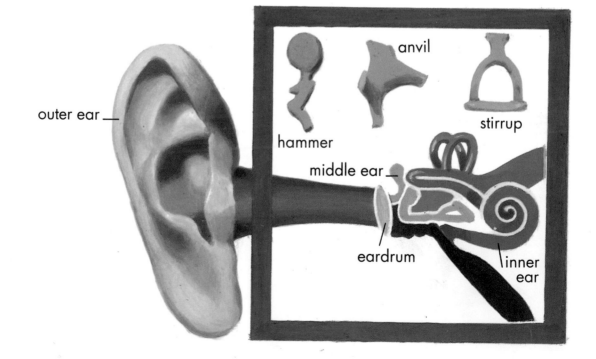

outer ear

anvil

stirrup

hammer

middle ear

eardrum

inner ear

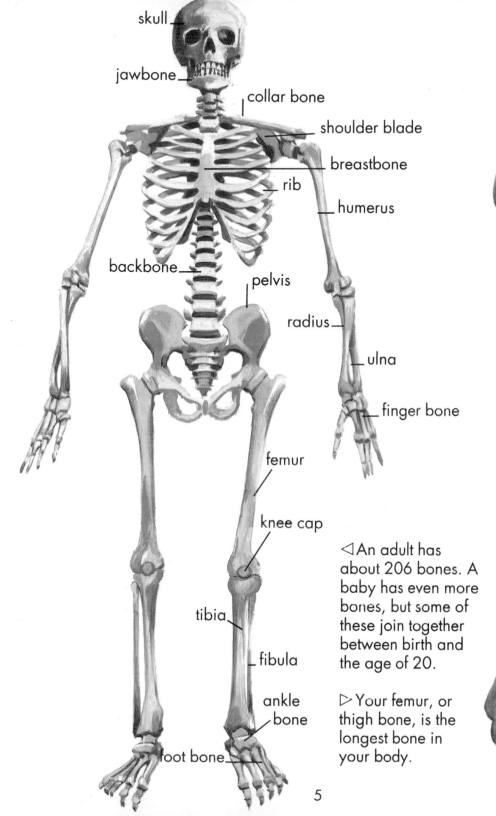

skull

jawbone

collar bone

shoulder blade

breastbone

rib

humerus

backbone

pelvis

radius

ulna

finger bone

femur

knee cap

tibia

fibula

ankle bone

foot bone

◁ An adult has about 206 bones. A baby has even more bones, but some of these join together between birth and the age of 20.

▷ Your femur, or thigh bone, is the longest bone in your body.

5

What are bones made of?

Bones are made of water and hard minerals, such as **calcium**. The outside of a bone is stiff and tough. But the inside is spongy and soft. This makes bones very strong but very light. They are covered in a special type of skin. If a bone breaks, the skin helps to make new bone to repair the crack. Some bones also contain jelly-like **bone marrow**. Red bone marrow makes new **red blood cells**.

▷ In an X-ray, the hard bones show up lighter. The dark parts are flesh.

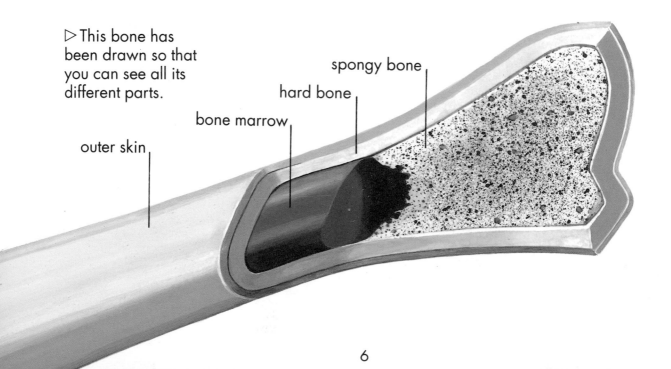

▷ This bone has been drawn so that you can see all its different parts.

spongy bone

hard bone

bone marrow

outer skin

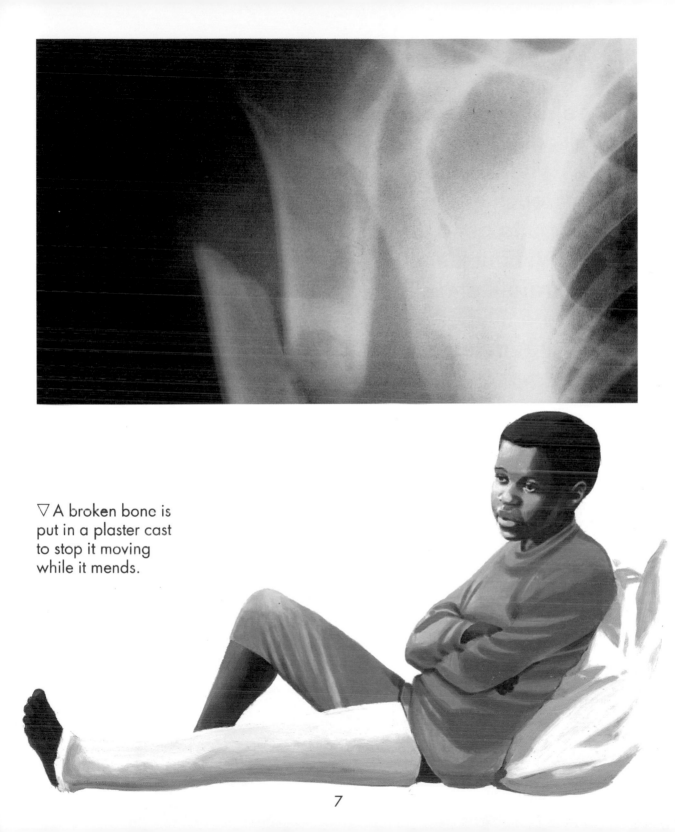

▽ A broken bone is
put in a plaster cast
to stop it moving
while it mends.

Joints

Your elbows, knees, shoulders and hips are all called movable joints. These are places where two bones meet but do not usually touch each other. Your joints allow you to bend, turn and twist your body. Without them, you would have to stand straight and stiff all the time. There are different types of joints. Each type moves in a different way.

▽There are about 100 moveable joints in your body. They let you move in many different ways. This gymnast has very supple joints.

8

△ Your elbow is a hinge and pivot joint. It opens and closes like a door hinge. It also rotates, or pivots, at one end.

▷ Your shoulder is a ball-and-socket joint. It lets your arm swing round.

◁ Lots of small bones make up the sliding joint in your ankle.

Inside a joint

The bones inside a joint are held in place by strong, stretchy straps. These are called **ligaments**. The ends of some bones are covered in rubbery **gristle** which is called cartilage. It stops the bones grinding together and wearing out. A special liquid keeps movable joints slippery and well oiled so that they work smoothly.

▷ Skiers put lots of strain on their knee joints. They often damage the cartilage inside.

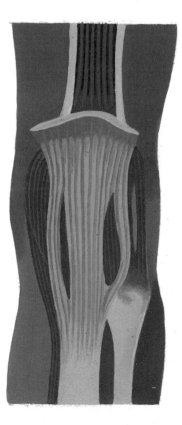

◁ Your knee joint is the biggest joint in your body. It is a hinge joint.

▷ A small bone protects the front of your knee joint. It is called your knee cap.

Your skull

Your skull is a hollow case of bones on top of your neck. One of its main jobs is to protect your brain. The bones in your skull are joined together like a jigsaw to make your skull stronger. Your bottom jaw is the only movable joint in your skull.

When you are born, some patches of your skull are soft and squashy. These knit together into hard bone as you grow older.

▽ Your skull is made up of a total of 22 bones by the time you are about 20. Most of these bones do not move.

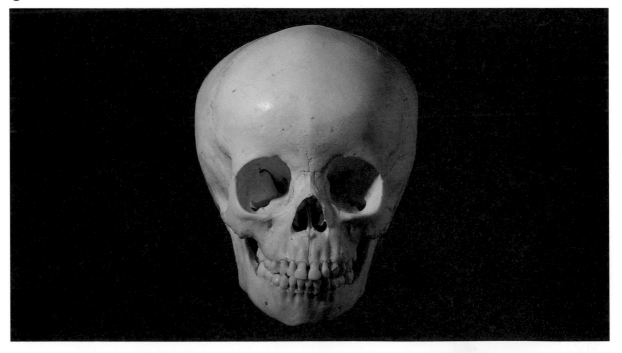

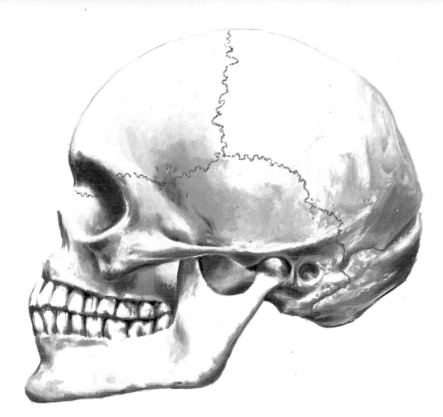

◁ The joins between the bones in your skull show up as zig-zag lines, called sutures.

fontanelles

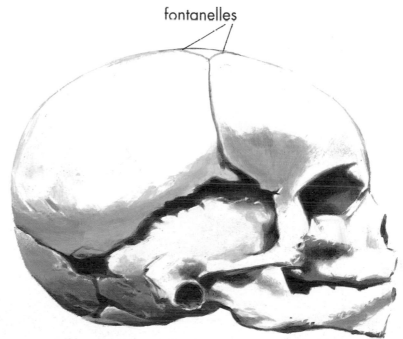

▷ A baby's skull is soft so it can easily squeeze out of its mothers' body, without being damaged, when it is born. It has special soft areas, called fontanelles, where the bones have not joined together.

13

Your backbone

A long chain of bones runs down your back. This is your backbone, or spine. It is made up of 26 bones, called **vertebrae**. Your spine is very strong but it can also bend so you can move. It supports your body and protects your **spinal cord**. This is a thick bundle of nerves running from your brain to your body. If your spinal cord is damaged, you can be **paralysed**.

▽ Your spine is slightly curved. This curve helps to protect the spine when you walk or run.

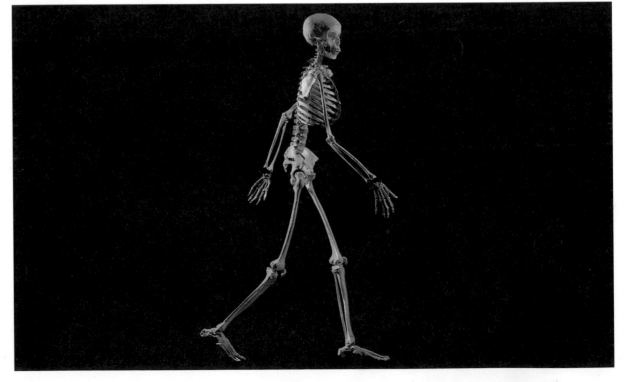

△ If you slump forwards when you sit, you may get back pains. It is better to sit with a straight back.

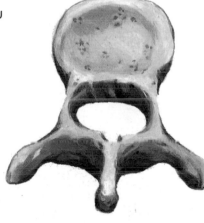

△ Each vertebra has a hole through the middle and three spikes. Your spinal cord runs through the hole. Muscles and ligaments are fixed to the spikes.

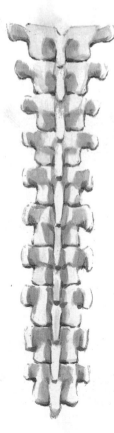

Main muscles

Hundreds of muscles lie under your skin. They work with your bones to make you move. The muscles are fixed to your bones by bands, called **tendons**. Clench your fist and pull it up towards your shoulder. Can you feel the muscles in your upper arm? Some muscles are big and powerful. Others are tiny and used for delicate movements. There are also muscles deep inside your body. They keep your heart beating and your lungs breathing.

▽ With exercise you can make your muscles bigger and stronger.

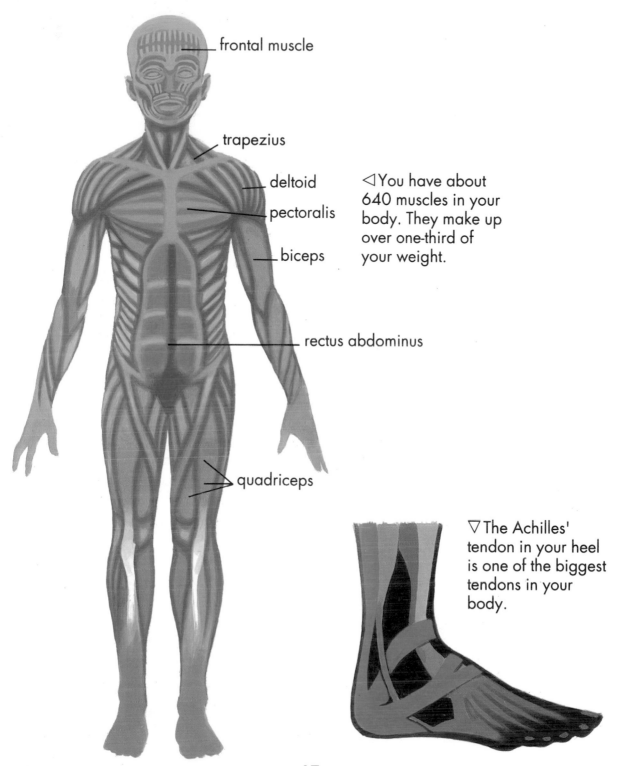

frontal muscle

trapezius

deltoid

pectoralis

biceps

rectus abdominus

quadriceps

◁ You have about 640 muscles in your body. They make up over one-third of your weight.

▽ The Achilles' tendon in your heel is one of the biggest tendons in your body.

Muscles at work

Your muscles pull on your bones to make you move. When you want to move your arm, your brain tells your arm muscles to get shorter, or **contract**. Muscles cannot push. They can only pull. So they often work in pairs. One muscle contracts to bend your arm. Then it relaxes and its partner contracts to straighten your arm again.

▷ Look at this weightlifter's arms. As the muscles contract, they get thicker and bulge.

biceps

triceps

△ Your biceps muscle contracts to bend your arm.

◁ Your triceps muscle contracts to straighten your arm.

Inside a muscle

A muscle is made of bundles of very fine **fibres**, like threads. A big muscle may have more than 2,000 fibres inside it. The fibres get shorter to give the muscle its pulling power. Each fibre is made up of even thinner threads. It also has nerves and blood running through it. The whole muscle is inside a stretchy covering.

▽ Your body has three different kinds of muscle.

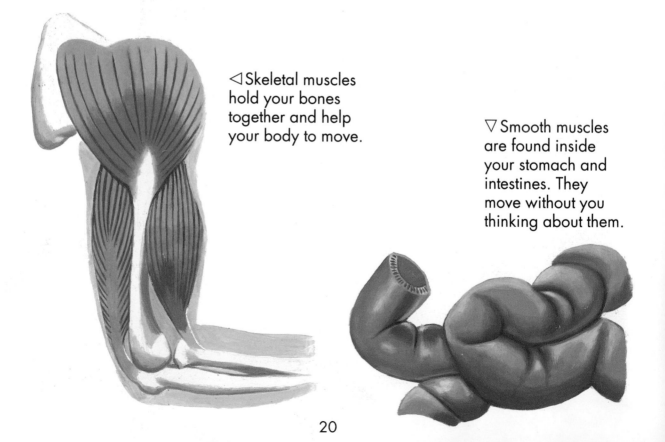

◁ Skeletal muscles hold your bones together and help your body to move.

▽ Smooth muscles are found inside your stomach and intestines. They move without you thinking about them.

▷ Your heart is made of a special type of muscle which never stops working. It is called cardiac muscle.

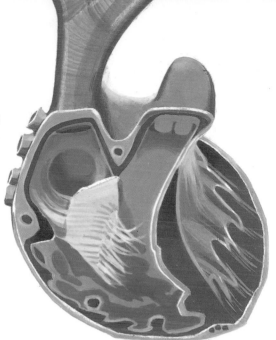

▽ Under a microscope, the fibres look like stripey bands.

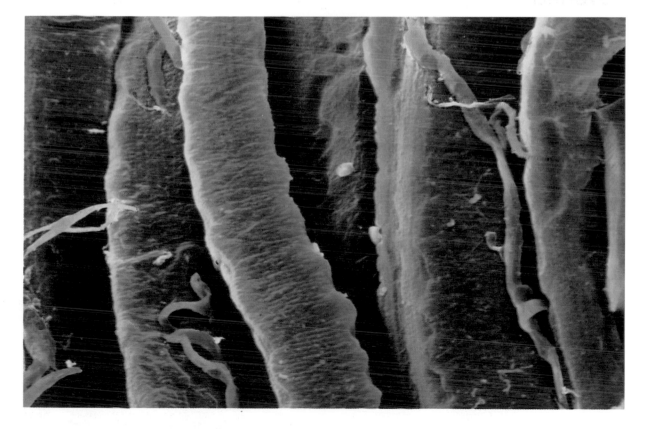

Fuel for muscles

Your muscles need **energy** to make them work. They get this energy from the food you eat and the air you breathe. Your blood carries the food and **oxygen** from the air to your muscle cells. Then the cells use the oxygen to release energy from the food. The harder your muscles have to work, the more energy they need.

▷During exercise, your muscles use up lots of energy. You may need to rest afterwards.

▽From time to time you may get cramp in a muscle. Stretch the muscle gently to ease the pain.

22

◁Always warm up before you take exercise and slow down gradually afterwards. This will stop your muscles aching.

Hands and arms

Think how often you use your hands and arms. And how many different ways do they move? The bones and muscles in your arms are big and strong for lifting and carrying. The bones and muscles in your hands are much smaller. They let you make lots of difficult and delicate movements. Your hands can pick up tiny things such as pins. They can also make complicated movements such as knitting or writing.

▽ Pianists do special exercises to make their fingers strong and supple.

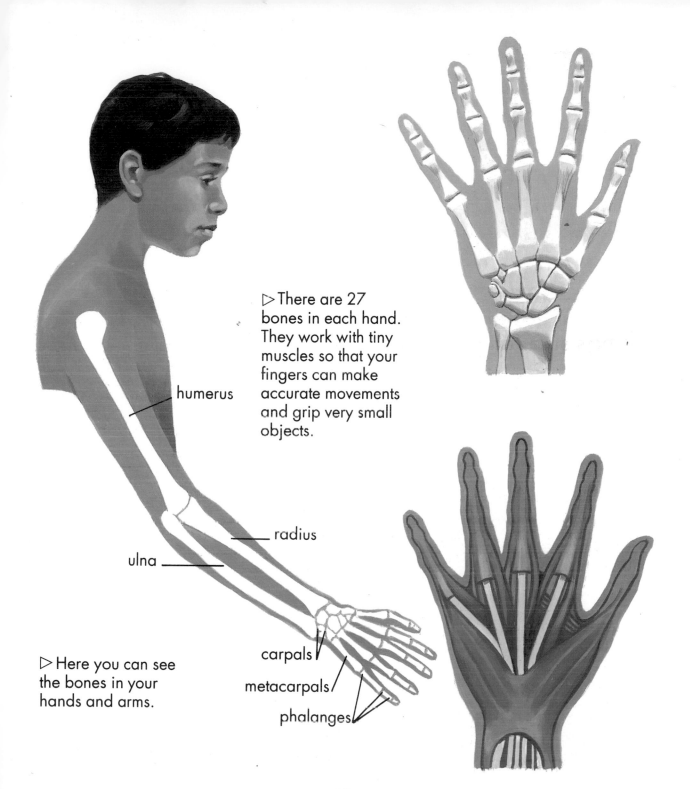

▷ There are 27
bones in each hand.
They work with tiny
muscles so that your
fingers can make
accurate movements
and grip very small
objects.

humerus

radius

ulna

▷ Here you can see
the bones in your
hands and arms.

carpals

metacarpals

phalanges

Legs and feet

Your legs and feet are built in a similar way to your arms and hands. But your legs are longer and stronger than your arms. This is because they have to support the weight of your body when you stand, walk or run about. The muscles and bones in your thighs are some of the biggest and most powerful in your whole body.

▷ Ballet dancers have very strong legs and feet for jumping and dancing on tip toe.

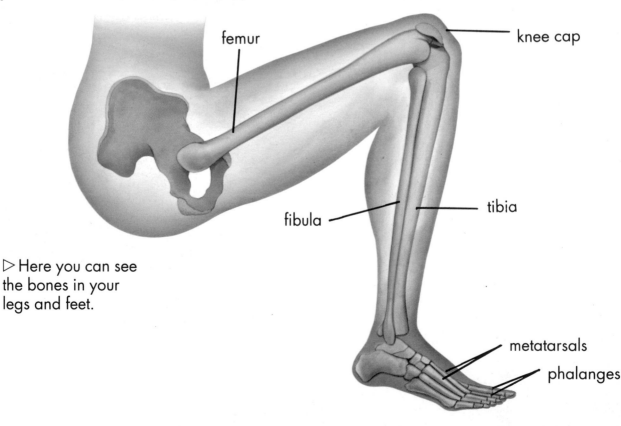

femur

knee cap

fibula

tibia

metatarsals

phalanges

▷ Here you can see the bones in your legs and feet.

Pulling faces

Look in the mirror and pull some faces. Raise your eyebrows, stick your tongue out, frown or smile. Each time you pull a face, you are using lots of different muscles. But these muscles do not pull on bones. They pull on your skin to make it move. The fastest-moving muscles are in your eyelids. They make you blink about 20,000 times a day.

▽ You can show people how you are feeling by the expression on your face.

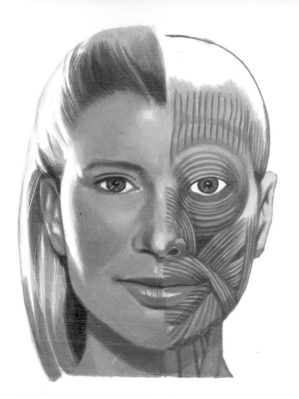

◁There are more than 30 muscles in your face. When you raise your eyebrows, you use most of these muscles.

Things to do

- The human body is very flexible. Can you make a list of as many different ways of moving as possible, such as bending, hopping and so on?

- Exercise is important for keeping your muscles and bones in good working order. Two of the best all-round types of exercise are swimming and cycling. They improve your strength, stamina and your suppleness.

- Always warm up before you exercise and slow down gently afterwards. This stops you tearing your muscles or becoming stiff.

Glossary

bone marrow A soft jelly inside your large bones. It makes new red blood cells and most white blood cells.

calcium A hard material which helps your bones to grow and to mend if they break. Your teeth and nails also contain calcium.

contract To get shorter or smaller.

energy The ability to move or work. Your body gets its energy from the food you eat.

fibre A fine thread.

gristle A tough, rubbery material.

ligament A strong, stretchy strap which holds bones in place.

oxygen A colourless gas which your body needs to keep it alive.

paralysed Unable to move.

red blood cell A part of your blood which carries oxygen around your body and gives your blood its colour.

skeleton The framework of bones inside your body.

spinal cord The thick bundle of nerves which runs from your brain down your back through your spine, or backbone.

tendon A band at the end of a muscle which fixes the muscle to a bone or another part of your body.

vertebrae The small bones which together make up the spine, or backbone, running down your back.

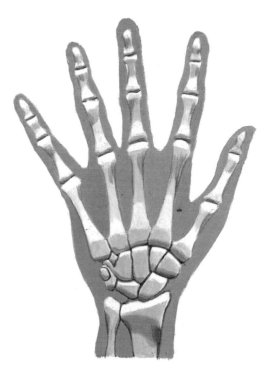

Index

Achilles' tendon 17
ankle 9
arms 16, 18, 19, 24–25

backbone 14–15
back pain 15
biceps 18
blood 6, 20
bone marrow 6, 31
bones 3, 4, 6–7, 10, 12, 14, 16, 20, 24, 25, 26
   broken 9
brain 3, 12, 14, 18

calcium 6, 31
cartilage 10
cells 22
cramp 22

ear 4
elbow 8, 9
energy 22, 31
exercise 16, 23, 30
eyelid 28

face 28, 29
feet 26–27
femur 4
fibre (muscle) 20, 31

gristle 10, 31

hands 24–25
heart 3, 16, 21
hip 8

jaw 12
joint 8–9, 10–11, 12

knee 8, 10

legs 26–27
ligament 10, 15, 31

muscle 3, 4, 15, 16–17, 18–19, 20–21, 22, 23, 24, 26, 28, 29

nerves 3, 14, 20

oxygen 22, 31

red blood cell 6, 31

shoulder 8, 9, 16
skeleton 4–5, 31
skin 16, 28
skull 12–13
spinal cord 14, 15, 31
spine 14, 15

triceps 18

vertebrae 14, 15, 31

Photographic credits:
Department of Clinical Radiology, Salisbury District Hospital/Science Photo Library 7, 13; Chris Fairclough Colour Library 8; Robert Harding Picture Library 11, 16; T. Hill 14, 28, 29; Prof. P.Motta/Dept. of Anatomy/ University 'La Sapienza'/Science Photo Library 21; ZEFA 3, 9, 12, 23, 24.